GONE WISHIN'!
A Funny Fill-ins Book

by Adam Beechen

SCHOLASTIC INC.

New York Toronto London Auckland Sydney
Mexico City New Delhi Hong Kong Buenos Aires

Based on the TV show *The Fairly OddParents*® created by Butch Hartman
as seen on Nickelodeon®

No part of this publication may be reproduced in whole or in part, or stored in a retrieval system
or transmitted in any form or by any means, electronic, mechanical, photocopying, recording,
or otherwise, without written permission of the publisher. For information regarding permission,
write to Simon Spotlight, Simon & Schuster Children's Publishing Division,
1230 Avenue of the Americas, New York, NY 10020.

ISBN 0-439-66666-X

Copyright © 2004 by Viacom International Inc. All rights reserved.
NICKELODEON, *The Fairly OddParents*, and all related titles, logos, and characters
are trademarks of Viacom International Inc. Published by Scholastic Inc.,
557 Broadway, New York, NY 10012, by arrangement with Simon Spotlight,
Simon & Schuster Children's Publishing Division.
SCHOLASTIC and associated logos are trademarks and/or registered
trademarks of Scholastic Inc.

12 11 10 9 8 7 6 5 4 3 2 1   4 5 6 7 8 9/0

Printed in the U.S.A.

First Scholastic printing, September 2004

TABLE OF CONTENTS

WHAT TO DO

FIRST get all of your friends together!

NOW pick one of those friends to tell the others what kinds of words are needed, and then to write their suggestions in the blanks. That friend will not read the section out loud until all of the blanks are filled in.

When your friend asks for a **NOUN**, fill in the name of a person, place, or thing. Some examples of nouns would be wand, baseball cap, and crown.

When your friend asks for a **VERB**, try to think of an action word, like wish, fly, or run. Sometimes you'll be asked for a past-tense verb. Words like wished, flew, and ran are past tense. And you'll also be asked for "-ing" words. This means words like wishing, flying, and running.

An **ADJECTIVE** is a word that describes a person, place, or thing, like crazy, scary, or excellent.

An **ADVERB** describes how something is done, and usually ends in "-ly," like scarily, easily, or happily.

Sometimes you'll be asked for something specific, like "animal," "kind of sandwich," or "number." Just fill in a word that's one of those things.

Wish you could get started? Turn the page and

LET'S GO!

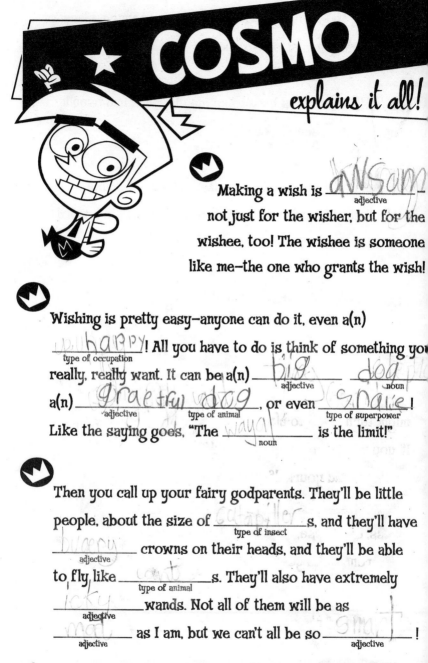

COSMO

explains it all!

Making a wish is _awsom_ (adjective) not just for the wisher, but for the wishee, too! The wishee is someone like me—the one who grants the wish!

Wishing is pretty easy—anyone can do it, even a(n) _happy_ (type of occupation)! All you have to do is think of something you really, really want. It can be a(n) _big_ (adjective) _dog_ (noun) a(n) _graetful_ (adjective) _dog_ (type of animal), or even _snake_ (type of superpower)! Like the saying goes, "The _waya_ (noun) is the limit!"

Then you call up your fairy godparents. They'll be little people, about the size of _catapiller_ (type of insect)s, and they'll have _buoory_ (adjective) crowns on their heads, and they'll be able to fly like _cat_ (type of animal)s. They'll also have extremely _loky_ (adjective) wands. Not all of them will be as _mat_ (adjective) as I am, but we can't all be so _smat_ (adjective)!

6

Now make your ___nail___. You can
noun

___run___ for whatever you want
verb

as long as you remember to say, "I

wish . . ." when asking your fairy

___but___ s for something. They
noun

will _____ their wands _____,
verb   adverb

and faster than you can say,

"_____." your wish
nonsense word

will be granted!

If you wish you could run faster,

your godparents might turn you

into a(n) _____. If you
type of animal

wish you could swim really well, they

might turn you into a(n) _____.
type of fish

If you wish to be rich, you could

suddenly find yourself with

___30___ bazillion dollars . . .
number

unless, of course, your ___happy___
adjective

godparents take your wish literally

and everyone starts calling you Rich

___Baks___!
last name of friend

When making a wish, you really have to _____
verb

your _____ to come up with something
noun

_____. One time Timmy wished he could
adjective

see through a(n) _____. I thought it would be
noun

more interesting for him to be able to see through

more than one _____ at a time, so I made it
same noun

so he could see through all _____s all the
same noun

time! Unfortunately Timmy found himself looking all

around the world until he couldn't see anything but his

own _____s!
noun

OKAY, MAYBE THAT'S A
BAD EXAMPLE.

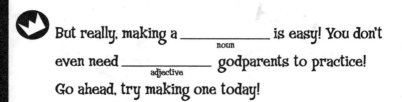

 But really, making a _____ is easy! You don't
noun

even need _____ godparents to practice!
adjective

Go ahead, try making one today!

Wanda

really explains it all!

What my _____ husband
           adjective
didn't mention is that there are some

other _____ things you need
           adjective
to know about wishing. We fairies

call them **"DA RULES."**

Da RULES

9

RULE # 1:

Fairies only grant wishes to kids! That means we can't
grant wishes to _____ s, _____
                 type of occupation   adjective
baby-sitters, or _____s. However, there are
                     type of animal
exceptions—like the time Timmy wished he were a
giant _____ so that he could scare the neighbor's
       type of animal
_____ dog, _____. Even though he
   adjective   pet's name
was a(n) _____ at the time, we turned him back
         same type of animal
into a kid again.

RULE # 2:

A kid with fairy godparents can't tell anyone they exist!
The second a kid spills the _____ s about his fairy
                     type of vegetable
godparents, they will disappear with a loud _____ ,
                                   sound effect
and they'll never come back!

RULE #3:

Fairy godparents aren't allowed to interfere with true love. Fairies are suckers for true love. The mere mention of it makes us _____ until our
___verb___

_____s turn _____!
___body part___   ___color___

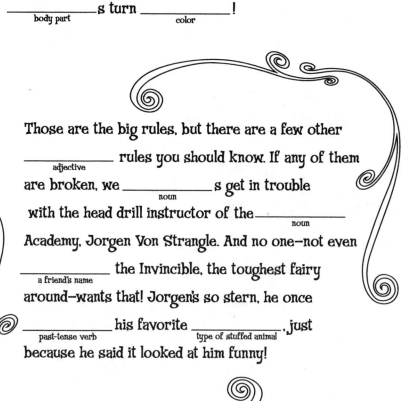

Those are the big rules, but there are a few other _____ rules you should know. If any of them
___adjective___

are broken, we _____s get in trouble
___noun___

with the head drill instructor of the_____
___noun___

Academy, Jorgen Von Strangle. And no one—not even

_____ the Invincible, the toughest fairy
___a friend's name___

around—wants that! Jorgen's so stern, he once

_____ his favorite _____, just
___past-tense verb___   ___type of stuffed animal___

because he said it looked at him funny!

RULE # 4:

Wishes can't be used to hurt anyone. But they *can* be used to embarrass someone! Is your classmate making fun of you? Why not wish for his _____ to suddenly be
<small>article of clothing</small>
filled with _____ ! Does the school bully keep
<small>type of liquid</small>
_____ you? Just wish for him to walk into
<small>-ing verb</small>
_____ wearing nothing but a(n) _____
<small>school subject</small> <small>article of clothing</small>
on his head. He may not stop bullying you, but you'll sure get a laugh!

RULE # 5:

Fairies can't help kids cheat. So we can't give you the answers when you're taking a _____ , but we
<small>noun</small>
can help you *find* the answers. If you've got a problem with your _____ homework, we can introduce
<small>school subject</small>
you to _____ , who knows all about it. And
<small>famous person</small>
if _____ can't _____ you, we can call
<small>same famous person</small> <small>verb</small>
_____ to teach you all about _____ s
<small>another famous person</small> <small>noun</small>
and _____ s in the blink of an eye.
<small>noun</small>

RULE # 6:

The wisher must be very careful and specific when wishing, otherwise all sorts of things might happen! For instance, Timmy once wished for the biggest _____ in the
_{junk food item}
whole world! Well, Cosmo and I conjured up a _____
_{same junk food item}
the size of _____! Timmy's whole neighborhood
_{U.S. state}
was filled with a(n) _____ smell for _____
_{adjective} _{number}
weeks! It took Timmy _____ wishes just to wish
_{number}
all of it away, and even then, there were still pieces of

_____ left in Timmy's mother's _____!
_{same junk food item} _{appliance}

Now that you *REALLY* know all there is

to know, we wish you

GOOD WISHING!

Dear Cosmo and Wanda

DEAR COSMO AND WANDA,

I am ___happy___ about last week's fiasco at the
    adjective

movies. If I had known things would have turned

out so _____, I never would have made the
        adverb

_____ in the first place!
    noun

It seemed like a **GREAT IDEA** at the time. I saw a

poster for the new movie, *The* _____
                                adjective

_____, and I just had to see it! I asked my
    noun

mom, but she said, **"TIMMY, YOU CAN'T SEE**

THAT. IT'S TOO _____ **!"**
                        adjective

I asked my dad, and he said,

"LISTEN TO YOUR

MOTHER, TIMMY.

She's one smart

_____ **!"**
    noun

Fairy World

That's when I came to you _____s . But
                                    noun
when you asked me if I would rather be **IN**

the movie, Cosmo, I thought it was a(n) _____
                                            adjective
idea . . . even though Wanda wasn't

so sure.

You waved your _____
                    adjective
wands, and suddenly I felt like I was

_____ , _____ , and
  -ing word   -ing word
_____ all at once!
  -ing word

ZAP! *GONE!* *ZAP!*

The next thing I knew, I was playing

the part of _____ , the _____
                silly name   adjective
_____ ! And I was right alongside
    noun
_____ , my **FAVORITE ACTOR!**
a male movie star

Together, we were supposed to search for the

_____ _____ , which had the power
  adjective   noun
to _____ _____s!
     verb   noun

Turn ➡

AT FIRST it was great and everything was going

_____. But we ran into some bad guys, and
_{adverb}

you could tell they were bad because they smelled like

rotten _____s!
_{type of vegetable}

I thought _____ would stay and fight them,
_{same male movie star}

but he turned out to be a big, frightened _____!
_{animal}

We ran and ran for what felt like _____ years!
_{number}

And I'm the slowest _____ in my class,
_{noun}

so I got tired really fast.

Finally, just as the bad guys were about to get me, I

decided being in movies isn't _____ after all!
                                    adjective

So when you showed up, I _____ to go back
                              past-tense verb

home! My costar was pretty upset when I left him to

face the bad guys alone. "Don't go, _____
                                          adjective

buddy," he begged. "These bad guys are going to

_____, _____, and _____ me!"
      verb   verb   verb

He cried like a(n) _____!
                        noun

So now I'm home, and I don't even

want to see the movie anymore

because I know now that my favorite

actor is a(n) _____ _____ ! All I
                 adjective   noun

wanted to do this weekend was see that movie. Now

I guess I'll have to do my _____ homework!
                                adjective

I WISH I'D NEVER MADE MY WISH!

Your _____ godson, Timmy
         adjective

THE FRANKLY FABULOUS FAIRY FINDER!

For a long time I wished someone would invent a _____
                                                       noun

that would help me prove fairies really exist! Well, my wish

came true! I just bought a Frankly Fabulous Fairy Finder,

and I think this will finally show people I'm not just some

_____ _____! Look what it says on the box.
adjective   noun

"THANK YOU FOR BUYING THE
FRANKLY FABULOUS FAIRY FINDER!
WE'RE __happy__ THAT YOU
         adjective
PURCHASED OUR PRODUCT, AND WE'RE
SURE YOU'LL FIND IT __Betful__,
                         adjective
__Defy__, AND __makeUP__!
adjective   adjective

If you don't find ___inride___ fairies in

_____ days, just return your Frankly
(number)

Fabulous Fairy Finder to _____ and we'll
(location)

give you a free _____!
(noun)

The Frankly Fabulous Fairy Finder is _____
(adjective)

and _____ to use. Simply put the pieces
(adjective)

together using a _____. Make sure all the
(noun)

pieces fit _____ together.
(adverb)

NOTE: The most important piece of the Fairy Finder is

the _____ _____! If it is not
(color) (noun)

installed _____, the machine will smell like
(adverb)

_____ _____s!
(adjective) (noun)

19

FABULOUS
FAIRY FINDER
DIRECTIONS

"When first activated, the Frankly Fabulous Fairy Finder

will _____ _____ . Do not be alarmed.
           verb   adverb

This is only the _____ heating up. Soon your Fairy
                        noun

Finder will be racing through the streets collecting fairies

like they were _____ s !
                    noun

"Once it has captured _____ fairies, the Fairy
                           number

Finder will store them in a giant _____ . Please
                                        noun

remember to feed your fairies lots of _____
                                           type of food

every _____ hours, or else they might turn into
          number

_____ _____ s.
   adjective   noun

"We hope you and your Frankly Fabulous Fairy Finder will be very _____ together. adjective Remember, the Fairy Finder needs _____ number nuclear-powered _____ s from the planet noun _____ , or it just won't work. Happy hunting! silly name

"Sincerely, the Frankly Fabulous Fairy Finder Company."

Now, if I could just figure out where _____ is same silly name and how to get my hands on some nuclear-powered _____ , I'd be able to prove the existence of same noun fairies and expose Timmy Turner once and for all. . . .

Vicky's

tips for baby-sitters

I know, you wish you could be as _____ as

                                    adjective

me, the most _____ baby-sitter that ever _____

              adjective   past-tense verb

a(n) _____!

      noun

Well, I put together a(n)

_____ list of

  adjective

things you need to

remember when

you baby-sit

to help you get through

the night.

From the desk of
Vicky
Baby-sitter

1. If the parents say their kid can go to bed at

_____ , you tell the kid he has to go to bed
time of day

at _____ ! That will show the twerp who's
time of day

boss!

2. Don't waste your time reading the same

_____ bedtime stories! Instead, make up a
adjective

scary story and call it "The _____
adjective

_____ that _____ the
noun   past-tense verb

_____ !" The kid will stay in bed all night
noun

with the covers pulled up to his _____ ,
body part

all freaked out!

3. Talk on the phone! You can call your

_____ , your _____ , and even your
relative   type of occupation

_____ in _____ ! It's not *your*
noun   foreign country

phone bill, so dial away!

23

4. If you want to keep the kid from telling his parents about how much you talked on the phone, make sure you put his _____ s all over the
noun
_____! If he squeals on you, you squeal on
a piece of furniture
him!

5. As the baby-sitter, you get to watch the TV shows *you* want to watch, not what the kids want to watch! My favorite shows are _____ s,
noun
_____ _____ s, and _____,
adjective   noun   exclamation
That's My _____ !
body part

6. Use the family's computer! You can do all kinds of _____ things: You can alter family photos
adjective
so it looks like the kid is _____ the _____
-ing verb   noun
from the _____ —in case you need to blackmail
noun
him later. You can go to gossip Web sites and find out
that _____ is dating _____. And you can
male movie star   female movie star
even do your homework . . . if you're really boring.

7. Invite your friends over! Throw a(n)

_____ party and eat all the family's _____ .
    adjective   type of food

Put a _____ CD on the stereo and play it really
        singer or band name

loud! Hold a skateboard contest in the _____ !
                                              type of room

8. If you want to keep the squirt quiet, tell him that if

he's not, you'll _____ until his _____
                      verb   noun

loses its _____ !
                noun

9. If the parents leave cookies for you to share with

the kid, and the cookies look really good, tell the kid that

cookies will make his _____ s _____ , and
                            body part   verb

that if he eats them, he'll turn into a(n) _____ !
                                                  type of animal

More cookies for you!

10. The most _____ thing to remember is,
                      adjective

no matter what happens, blame the twerp!

HOW TO HANDLE

your baby-sitter

Don't listen to Vicky! She's a totally

__Men__ __Pigheoo__ !
adjective _type of animal_

If you're stuck with a(n)

__Men__ baby-sitter, and you
adjective

wish you knew what to do about it,

take this advice from me:

When she tells you to be quiet, __be__ as loud as
verb

you can!

When the baby-sitter won't let you watch the TV shows

you want to watch, take her favorite __800__ s,
noun

and tell her you won't give them back for __800__
number

years unless she lets you watch your favorite cartoon,

__happy TV__ , the Magic __Cdtoon__
adjective _noun_ _noun_

Reprogram the computer so that when she tries to use it, the screen says, "__go__ ! "
exclamation

If she tries to make you go to bed early, reset all the clocks so they say it's __8am__ o'clock—way ahead of your bedtime!
time of day

Tie _____s to the
noun
baby-sitter's shoes when she's not looking.

Use her lipstick to __blak__
verb
a pretty __back__ .
noun

Ask your fairy godparents to turn the baby-sitter into a _____ until
kitchen appliance
your __moms__ come home!
noun

GET IN SHAPE WITH DAD

When you _____ around as much
                verb
as I do, trying to get everything done, you

need   to be in _____ shape!
                              adjective
That's why I came up with the

perfect workout routine!

STEP 1: Always make sure you're wearing

proper exercise clothing! That means a(n)

_____ , a good pair of _____ s,
article of clothing   noun
and a brightly colored _____ on your head!
                              noun

STEP 2: Stretching is very important! If you

don't stretch, you could really _____
                                      verb
your _____ ! I suggest stretching for at
        noun
least _____ minutes before you
            number
start exercising.

STEP 3: Get your heart pumping! Try jumping up and down

on a _____. Or run _____ miles around your
      noun   number

_____.
   noun

STEP 4: Work those muscles! Remember to do your

_____ lifts, your _____ crunches and your
  body part   body part

_____ twists!
  body part

STEP 5: Eat healthy! A good workout means nothing without

proper nutrition. So after you exercise, have a big bowl of

_____s, have a _____ drenched in
 type of vegetable   type of food

_____, maybe a few_____s and wash it all down
 type of liquid   type of fruit

with a big glass of _____. Yummy!
             type of liquid

Just stick to this routine for a good_____
                                 number

weeks, and your body will be as _____
                                 adjective

as mine!

Gardening

WITH

MOM

I wish I knew why I can't grow anything in my garden! I think I'm doing all the right things, but it's hard to tell.

❀ I know my __daisy__ needs lots of
type of plant
__water__, so I make sure to put it in
noun
my _____ .
location

❀ Plants need water, and lots of it! I try to give my plants __80__ gallons of
number
water a day, and I water them with my

_____ !
noun

🌸 Nobody likes getting on their hands and knees to pull weeds, so I use a _____ to do the work for me!

type of tool

🌸 I've been trying to grow_____, but the

type of vegetable

_____s that live in our neighborhood keep

type of animal

eating them! So I've put up a scarecrow that looks

like _____. That should scare them away!

name of teacher

🌸 I like trimming my plants so they look like people or animals! I shaped one plant to look like a(n)

_____ _____, and another to look

adjective   *type of animal*

like _nancy_. But I think I made the _____

famous person   *body part*

too big.

🌸 Maybe I'll never be good at gardening. But at least I have fun doing it!

Big Bully Blues

Last week I got so tired of Francis picking on me at

_____, I made a _____ to try and change
    location   noun

things. But I really wish I hadn't!

Francis is the toughest kid in my school.

He's meaner than a cage of _____
                                     adjective

_____s. He's bigger than a
   type of animal

giant _____ and about as
         noun

smart. He's repeated the same

grade _____ times!
        number

Even the teachers are afraid of him!

Francis calls me _____ face,
adjective
and he calls Chester Mr. _____.
adjective
When he's not calling us names, he's

threatening to beat us up if we don't

give him our _____s. And he
noun
only does it because he's bigger

than us!

I decided I was tired of being treated like a(n)

_____ _____. So I told Cosmo and Wanda
adjective   noun

I wished I were bigger than Francis. "A little bigger or a

lot bigger?" Cosmo asked. I figured that being a lot

bigger would be a lot better, so that's what I said!

My fairy godparents _____ waved their
                        adverb

_____ wands, and–_____! I started to
adjective   sound effect

grow and grow and grow some more! The next thing I

knew I was _____ feet tall!
                number

POOF!

I was pretty _____ at first and I ran right
                  adjective
over to find Francis. Of course, I was so big that I

stepped on lots of _____, _____, and
                        nouns   nouns
_____ along the way—but I didn't care. All I
   nouns
wanted to see was Francis's _____ face when
                                 adjective
I knocked _____ on his door!
              adverb

When he saw me, Francis was so scared he nearly

_____! He promised not to bother me again.
past-tense verb
Being big was _____!
                  adjective

But I found out there was a downside. Not only was

Francis scared of me but so was everyone else! I was so

big, I couldn't control my _____ arms and legs, and
                            adjective

I kept _____ things over, like buildings! I almost
       -ing verb

knocked over my own house! I felt like the creature in

Attack of the _____ *-Foot Monster!*
                   number

I wished for Cosmo and Wanda to make me my normal size again.

But I probably should have asked to be made just a little bit bigger than Francis! The minute Francis saw I was back to normal, he _____ his knuckles and
past-tense verb
smiled _____ .
adverb
"WELCOME BACK, _____
adjective
FACE," he said. Uh-oh!

A.J.'S amazing FACTS

Indubitably, my knowled[ge]

base is extensive. Tha[t]

means I know a lot. My brain ho[lds]

_____ facts. And I alwa[ys]
  big number

wish I knew more. Here are just

a few of the interesting things I

know:

The _____ in _____ is _____ feet
       landmark   location   number

tall and is completely filled with _____ .
                                      type of food

The fastest _____ on Earth can go _____
              type of vehicle   number

miles per hour. And it only has three _____ !
                                           nouns

_____ discovered _____ in
a famous person   *country*

_____ .
year

There are _____ bones in the human
                number

_____ . If you break any of them while _____ ,
body part   *-ing verb*

a(n) _____ can fix them using a _____ .
     type of occupation   *type of tool*

_____ s have a highly developed sense of
type of animal

_____ . And they can _____ for more than
noun   *verb*

_____ minutes!
number

_____ is played with a _____ and a
type of sport   *noun*

_____ , and the object is to put the _____
noun   *noun*

in the _____ . The game was invented by _____
       noun   *a friend's name*

as a way of _____ his _____ s.
             -ing verb   *body part*

$$E = A.J.^2$$

THE CRIMSON CHIN'S *greatest adventures*

I know you've read all of my comic book adventures,
but some of the most _____ never made it to
                           adjective
the page! By my mother's mandible, I wish you could
have read them . . . I remember them like they
happened _____ days ago. . . .
             number

y partner, Cleft the Boy Chin Wonder,

nd I battled the Bronze Kneecap in an

venture I call "My _____.
                        noun

ly Enemy!" I thought for sure we were

eaten when the Kneecap trapped us in

giant _____! But Cleft used
            noun

_____ to break us out of
      noun

ur trap with a huge _____!
                          sound effect

fter that, I took care of the Kneecap

ith a(n) _____ shot
              adjective

o the _____!
            body part

POW!

took on a(n)_____ new supervillain, the_____
                adjective   adjective
_____, in a story called, "All My _____s Against
type of animal   noun
le!" The _____ _____ hypnotized every
            same adjective   same type of animal
_____ in the city, making them _____ like
type of occupation   verb
_____s! I destroyed the hypnotist with my _____
      noun   type of tool
nd got a free _____ as my reward!
                     noun

I BATTLED THE LEGION OF EVIL _____
                                adjective
_____ S IN A TALE EVERYONE CALLED,
    noun

"IF THIS BE _____ !"
              day of the week

The Legion used a _____ to
                      noun

_____ turn all the _____ s
  adverb   noun

in the city into _____
                   -ing verb

_____ s. It took all my _____
  noun   adjective

_____ s to get everything back to
  noun

normal!

I faced my greatest challenge in

"Attack of the _____
                 adjective

Monster from Planet _____!"
                        sound effect

The monster had _____
                      color

_____s all over his body,
    noun

and his breath smelled like

_____s! It wanted to eat
type of vegetable

every _____it could find!
         type of car

Luckily, I realized it was

allergic to _____,
              type of food

and after I fed it some, the

creature started to

_____ like a(n)
    verb

_____! Earth was
    noun

saved again, and everyone

cheered, "Crimson Chin,

you're our_____
               adjective

_____!"
    noun

FAIRY ACADEMY APPLICATION FORM

So . . . you wish you could join the Fairy Academy, yes? Well, let me tell you something: It is not easy!

No, it is very _____ !
_{adjective}

How _____ you ask?
_{same adjective}

Just look at the Fairy Academy Application Form—if you're not too much of a wimpy _____
_{noun}

—and you'll see what I mean!

PERSONAL INFORMATION:

My name is _____ _____ _____ .
                  sound effect   type of fruit   body part

My address is _____ _____ Lane.
               number   kind of tree

My birthday is _____ _____, _____ .
             month   big number   really big number

I have _____ brothers, _____ sisters, and one
      number   number

_____ .
noun

PHYSICAL SKILLS:

I can lift _____ sacks of _____ s over my head.
        number   noun

I can run _____ miles with _____
        number   adjective

_____ s chasing me.
noun

When I flex my _____ s, I can knock over
          body part

heavy _____ s .
      noun

45

Before wanting to join the Fairy Academy, I worked as

a _____ . I left that job because it was too
    noun

_____ .
   adjective

I have studied such subjects as _____ ,
                                        noun

_____ , and _____ . I can also say, "I am
      noun   noun

a(n) _____ , _____ _____ ,"
         adjective   adjective   noun

in _____ .
   foreign language

I have many _____ skills. I can _____ ,
                 adjective   verb

_____ , and _____ , and in the kitchen I
     verb   verb

make a mean _____ salad. The key is to add lots
               type of food

of _____ s!
      noun

PERSONAL GOALS AND PHILOSOPHY:

_____ years from now, I hope to be _____
    number   -ing verb

in _____, helping _____s with their
      country   occupation

_____s.
   animal

I have always wanted to join the Fairy Academy because I

think it would be _____ to help kids wish for
                              adjective

_____s, _____s, and _____ s.
  noun   noun   noun

I believe that _____ work and complete
                  adjective

_____can make a person _____.
  noun   adjective

I promise to never let a _____ get in the way of
                           animal

my _____ duty as a _____ student at the
     adjective   adjective

Fairy Academy.

POOF

ONE LAST WISH . . .

Now that you've finished filling in all

the blanks in this ___fan___
                      adjective

book, I wish you and your friends

would ___go___ back to the
          verb

beginning and ___DO it___ again.
                    verb

POOF!